HOMESTEAD
A NEW LIFE ON MARS

BY A.L. COLLINS
ILLUSTRATED BY TOMISLAV TIKULIN

raintree

a Capstone company — publishers for children

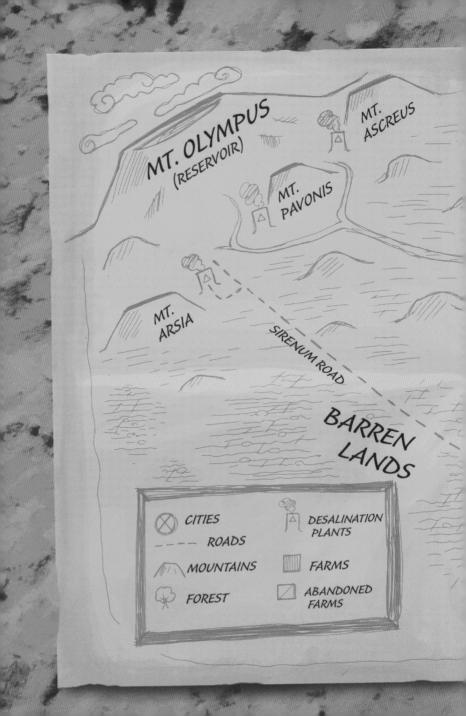

OLYMPIA PROVINCE
THARSIS CITY
N
W
E
S
FERRY LANDING
MARINE VALLEY RIVER
SUN VALLEY ROAD
TA'AL'S HOUSE
SUN CITY
SCHOOL
AONIA ROAD
OUR FARM
WALKER FARM
RAIDERS!
DARWIN CITY

Belle Song

Twelve-year-old Belle can be headstrong and stubborn. Her curiosity and sense of adventure often get her into trouble. Still, she has a good heart and is passionate about fairness. She is fiercely loyal to her friends.

Yun and Zara Song

Belle's parents sometimes seem really strict. But Yun has a great sense of humour, which Belle both loves and is embarrassed by. Zara has a generous heart, which has taught Belle not to judge others too quickly.

Melody

Melody is an old model 3X Personal Home Helper android. She was given to Belle by her grandmother before she passed away. Melody is Belle's best friend and protector, and enjoys telling bad jokes to seem more human.

MAIN INHABITANTS

Lucas Walker

Lucas is Belle's neighbour and classmate. He is part Sulux and part human. Meeting new people is not easy for him. But once he knows someone, his adventurous side emerges. He is full of ideas, which sometimes gets him and his friends into trouble.

Ta'al

Ta'al and her family are Nabian, an ancient alien race from another star system. Born and raised on Mars, Ta'al is intelligent and curious. She enjoys exploring and adventure, and quickly becomes Belle's closest friend on Mars.

It is the year 2335. Life on Earth is very difficult. Natural resources such as trees, water and oil are nearly gone. Many animal species have become extinct, and air pollution is causing widespread disease. More than 50 years ago, intelligent robots rose up to overthrow their human creators. After the Robot Rebellion ended, people were terrified of advanced technology. Many Terrans, those who are from Earth, chose to avoid robots and returned to a more basic lifestyle. But a few families still use less advanced robots as companions for their children.

Many people moved to the Moon to begin a new life on Lunar Colony. But it is overcrowded and has limited resources. Other families chose to move to Mars instead. With the help of two alien races – the Sulux and the Nabians – the red planet was transformed to support life nearly 200 years ago.

Hoping to find a better life, Yun and Zara Song and their daughter, Belle, have used all their savings to make the move to Mars. But as soon as they arrive, they learn that their new jobs with the Belt Asteroid Mining Corporation (or BAMCorp) have been eliminated by the company.

What will the Songs do now? They can't return to Earth, where nothing but hardship awaits them. Their only option is to find a way to build a new life on . . .

REDWORLD

CHAPTER ONE
:STUCK ON MARS:

"So we came all the way to this planet for nothing?"

Belle couldn't believe their bad luck. The Song family had sold all of their belongings and flown to Mars to start a new life. Her parents had been so excited about their new jobs with BAMCorp . . . and now those jobs were gone.

"Made redundant." Whatever that meant. Those were the words used by the company's representative.

"What do we do now?" Belle's mum, Zara, pressed her hands to her temples in frustration.

"BAMCorp gave us a week's stay in a hotel here in Utopia. They'll pay for the return trip too. Bah!" Her dad, Yun, exhaled loudly. "Some comfort that is!"

"I believe you are using sarcasm," Melody, Belle's android companion and best friend, chimed in. "Would a joke help to make you feel better?"

Belle nudged her. Melody often said the wrong thing at the wrong time in her quest to be more human. Secretly, Belle was happy that they'd be going back to Earth. She had never wanted to move in the first place.

"Let's go to the hotel, then," Belle said. She was careful not to sound too cheerful.

Zara sighed. She pulled her long hair back into a ponytail and put on her brave smile.

"The hotel can wait," she said. "On the way here, I saw a lively marketplace. Why don't we do some exploring first?"

Outside the corporation's big, black gates, the Song family was attacked by dust. Red, hot dust. Belle sneezed uncontrollably. Melody's white body became a dusty rust colour in a matter of seconds.

The red dust was everywhere. People kicked it into the air as they walked. Transports created giant dust clouds with their wheels. Low flying shuttles whipped up even more. There was so much dust that the sky looked brown and rusty. And there wasn't a single tree to be seen. This was why Earth people rarely moved to Mars.

"Isabelle Song! Keep up," Zara called. "We don't want to lose you in this crowd."

"Coming." Belle rolled her eyes. She hated it when her parents used her full name.

The market was crowded. Row upon row of makeshift stalls were crammed together. The fabric roofs flapped in the breeze as merchants shouted to people passing by.

"Finest meal-worm flour this side of Mars!"

"Most tender meat you'll ever taste!"

"Scarves of all colours – buy two, get one free!"

People filled the alleys, making bargains and shouting at each other. Melody shuffled along next to Belle. Zara stopped at one stall and bought scarves for herself and Belle to wrap around their heads. Melody got one too. Belle tied it around her android's neck joint to help keep the dust out.

"You look just like a Martian girl," Zara said. But Belle didn't want to be a Martian girl. She was Terran and couldn't wait to get back to Earth.

The scarf did help Belle to breathe more easily though. She relaxed enough to enjoy looking at the merchants' stalls.

She was struck by all the smells – roasted meats mixed with flowery perfumes. It made her stomach grumble and her nose tickle at the same time. Walking through the market, she was drawn to a stall that sold antique books.

"Diaries . . . these are rare back on Earth," Zara said, picking up a soft, brown, leather-bound book. On the front cover was an engraved image of the first human ship ever to land on Mars. "No one writes on paper anymore."

"It is not real paper, Zara," Melody corrected. "Even on Earth, there are not enough trees left to make the original product. This is 3D-printed, imitation paper."

Zara smiled at the android. Belle thought the diary was fantastic, especially the spaceship on the cover.

"Can I use my pocket money to buy this?" she asked.

"Do you know what a diary is?"

Belle laughed. "Of course I do. I record log entries through Melody all the time."

"It's quite different using paper and pen. Writing and drawing on paper is an ancient art form," Zara said. "But if you promise to give writing a try, you may purchase it."

Belle bargained the price down until the seller's face turned a bright red. She even got him to throw in a pencil for free. After she pressed her finger to his datapad to pay, she realized that they had lost sight of her dad. Melody extended her neck to stretch her head up about a metre higher in the air. This was one android ability that Belle sometimes wished she had. It was very useful for finding people and things. Everything Melody could see was projected onto the screen on her torso, so Belle could search for her dad too. Within seconds, they found him.

Melody led Belle and her mum past several market stalls, squeezing past clusters of people until they reached the middle of the market. Yun was leaning up against a stall, talking to a woman who was wrapped up in so many scarves that all Belle could see were her eyes.

Yun greeted his family with a huge grin. It was the first time Belle had seen him smile since they'd landed on Mars.

"I've found the solution to our problems," he said, spreading his arms open wide. "We're going to be farmers!"

It took several seconds for the news to sink in. Belle had just been looking forward to going back to Earth and telling her friends about her visit to the red planet. This was a whole different story.

"That's wonderful!" Zara said. "Farming's been in my family for generations. Up until my parents' time, that is, when they moved to the city."

So mum is excited too? Belle thought worriedly.

"Farms are located on the other side of Mars," Yun explained. "There's a lot of land to be had. The possibilities are endless."

"The region is called Olympia, after the big volcano," the woman at the stall said. "Locals call it the Wild West."

"It'll be an adventure," Yun said. "It's just the thing we Songs need."

Belle looked at her dad, then at her mum. Zara was looking at Yun as though he was her hero. Melody was busy scanning the woman in the scarves. Nobody could see how ridiculous this idea was.

Nobody but Belle.

Earth Date: 13 March 2335
Mars Day 1, summer

We're going to be farmers?
Let me tell you a secret. No one in the Song family can even keep a cactus alive for more than a week. On Earth, we lived in a city apartment and didn't even have a garden! Dad has never even mowed a lawn. Mum is allergic to cats! We don't know the first thing about growing crops or taking care of animals.

How are we going to survive here as farmers?

end.

CHAPTER TWO
JOURNEY TOWARDS A NEW LIFE

"Three tickets to Darwin!" Yun waved the tickets in the air, as he walked into their hotel room the next morning.

"Darwin?" Belle said, stretching out in her comfy bed. "I thought Tharsis City was the capital of the Olympia region."

"Darwin is the second largest city in Olympia," Yun pointed to the small map printed on the back of the ticket. "They say it's about half the size of the capital. And it's in the south, where we're going."

"We'll stop in Darwin to pick up supplies," Zara added. "Then we go on to Sun City, where our farm is."

"That's too many cities to keep track of," Belle grumbled. The geography of Mars was so confusing.

Her dad laughed. "We're new here. By the end of summer, it'll all be as familiar as home."

Belle's heart sank. Mars would never be home. She half-hoped this crazy plan would fail so they could return to Earth. That would be embarrassing, but it was better than starving to death in the middle of nowhere.

"The transport departs in one hour," Melody's joints squeaked from all the dust that coated her legs.

They checked out of the BAMCorp hotel and made their way through the market to the other side of town. Belle hiked her pack higher up on her back and followed her parents. It took a lot of effort to get used to the lower gravity on Mars. Each footstep took her higher off the ground than she wanted, so she had to adjust her pace.

The heat added to Belle's grumpiness. Her scarves were glued to her face with sweat. When she'd finally peeled the last scarf off, she was standing in the middle of the noisy Utopia Transit Station.

Belle gaped at the cavernous building. Giant pillars held up the corrugated roof. Shuttles of all sizes lined up on one side of the station like huge hibernating animals. On the other side were the land vehicles – some resembled ordinary Earth buses, and others looked like flying boats.

"Those are hover buses," Melody explained. "They are faster and more comfortable than the wheeled ones."

"Come on." Yun jogged towards what looked like a gigantic lifeboat crossed with a catamaran. It had windows all along its sides, and three pairs of propellers attached to engines on top. Smaller land transports rumbled onto the craft and disappeared into its midsection, while people lined up to enter via one of two ramps. "That's our shuttle."

Belle and Melody were the last passengers to climb the ramp. As Belle stepped into the main cabin, she was hit by the stench of sweaty bodies. She quickly re-wrapped her soggy scarves over her mouth and nose, and then squeezed onto the last available bench with her parents.

"Androids belong in the next compartment." A man in uniform pointed at Melody. "Strap yourself to a wall port."

As the shuttle ramp clanked and wheezed itself closed, the engines began to rumble. The air around Belle grew warm and stale. She felt dizzy.

"I think I'm going to be sick," she said.

A large woman sitting at the end of their row looked alarmed. "First time on a shuttle?"

Belle nodded.

The woman slapped her thighs and snorted. Belle could smell her onion breath all the way down the bench. It made her gag. The woman rose out of her seat.

"Sit down!" yelled the uniformed man.

"Keep yer britches on!" she yelled back. "I'm trying to prevent an incident here."

The woman scooted past three other passengers, and signalled to Belle's family to stand up. Was she kicking them off the flight?

Belle opened her mouth to protest, but then the woman waved the Songs over towards her seat by the window. She also ordered everyone else on their bench to move over in the other direction.

"Can't have this young one up-chucking on us all, can we?" she said with a grin. One of her teeth was black, which made her look like she had a gap in her mouth. "Come along, newbies. The view will make yer forget the sickness."

Zara thanked the woman so many times that Belle felt embarrassed for her mum.

Sitting by the open window did help the dizziness. As the shuttle rose into the air, a gentle breeze fanned her warm face. It lulled her into a much needed nap.

Hours later, Belle was woken by her dad nudging her.

"Look, Belle. You've got the best view of the land below."

The shuttle had long left the Utopian plains behind. They were now flying low over the outer lands. Yun leaned over her, craning to see out of the window.

"That's the three Terras below."

"The three terrors?" Belle asked.

He laughed. "No, *Terras*. It's the way people once referred to regions on Mars. These days they're known by their modern names – Araba, Saba and Meridian."

"I've never heard those names." Belle had studied maps of Mars on the flight from Earth. She had a good memory for names. But these were unfamiliar.

"That's probably because no one can live in these three regions," Yun said. "If you look carefully, you might spot the remains of old terraforming machines. No one knows why terraforming didn't work here."

The red planet had been transformed about two hundred years earlier. Before the terraforming machines did their work, Mars didn't have enough air or water to support human life.

Belle stared at the dry, reddish-brown land below her. "It's nothing but desert."

"You can't see it, but right now we're flying over an underground river that starts in the mountains and ends at Lake Hellan. It's actually the deepest crater on Mars."

"Cool! But how do farmers grow anything here?"

"There!" Yun pointed ahead. "That's how!"

It was as if someone had drawn a line in the ground. Suddenly the red dusty land transformed into spaces of brilliant greens and blues. Even the sky seemed to change colour, and there were clouds.

Belle gasped so loudly that several other passengers chuckled. Below her was a completely different planet.

"You see that big river?" Yun said. "The underground one rises to meet it. That's the Marine Valley River. Several smaller rivers join it at different points to the west."

"It's beautiful," Belle said. "And so blue!"

"Yes, but it's also very salty water," Zara added. "That's why you'll see huge buildings alongside the rivers. We can't drink salt water, so those desalination plants purify it for us."

Yun then pointed to three large mountains in the distance. "Those are extinct volcanoes," he said. "Terraforming changed them into water reservoirs to hold the planet's most precious resource – purified water. And those giant buildings are the desalination plants."

"There's a bigger mountain even further out," Zara said. "Can you see it?"

Belle squinted through the low clouds. She could only make out a large shadow looming behind the three closer volcanoes.

"That's Mount Olympus," Yun said. "It's the biggest volcano, not just on Mars, but in the entire solar system."

"I suppose that's why they called this part of Mars Olympia, huh, Dad?"

"You're absolutely right, Belle."

A loud voice crackled through the shuttle speakers, announcing that they were about to land in Darwin. The shuttle bumped and jostled as it descended through the windy layers of air. Finally, it dropped onto the landing pad with a sharp thud. Every passenger let out a loud sigh.

"Let's go and find our new farm!" Yun said. He and Zara hurried off the shuttle.

Belle waited for Melody, her only friend on this strange new world. Together, they stepped onto the soil of Olympia.

Earth Date: 14 March 2335
Mars Day 2, summer, evening

This has been the longest day of my life. When I woke up two days ago, we were going to live in Utopia and my parents were going to work for BAMCorp. All the photos Dad showed me made it seem that life on Mars would be great. Even the company's hotel was fantastic.

But here we are in the middle of nowhere — Darwin, Olympia. Yes, the flight over was interesting. I've never seen such big volcanoes so close together. I admit, the landscape is amazing. One moment it looks like desert, the next, it looks like Earth.

But Darwin is a poor and dusty version of Utopia. It's so backward. There are no tall buildings or aircars like the ones we have at home. It reminds me of an ancient western town in those old cowboy films Dad likes to watch.

Dad says it's too late to go on to Sun City, where our new farm is. So he got us a hotel room for the night. It's nothing like the BAMCorp hotel from last night. The video-wall doesn't even have Earth programming. I'm stuck watching some boring documentary about who came to Mars first. Who cares?

CHAPTER THREE

HOMEWARD BOUND

Morning in Darwin dawned bright and hot. The heat
rose from the ground and beat down from above at the
same time. Belle felt like she was part of a heat sandwich.

She held on to Melody's hard fingers as they followed
Yun and Zara out of the hotel and into the streets of
Darwin. The noise of transport craft and shouting voices
gave Belle a headache.

Yun led the family to a large shop. The sign outside
read Guntar's Emporium. Once inside, Belle felt better. It
was cooler and quieter in here. She wandered through the
aisles, looking at all the pretty things in the "luxury items"
section. There were beautifully decorated plates and lacy
fabric that she didn't dare to touch. In another section she
marvelled at ancient books that were made out of actual
paper. She pulled one gently off the shelf, slid to the floor,
and began to read.

● ● ● ●

"It is time to go," Melody interrupted. Belle blinked up
at her android. "You have been sitting here for two hours."

How had so much time passed without her realizing it?
She reluctantly replaced the book on the shelf and followed
Melody outside.

There, in front of the shop, were her parents, loading
up an old, rusted wagon.

"What's this old thing?" Belle blurted.

Yun wiped his forehead with his sleeve. "It's all we
could afford. At least it moves."

"It is a Mark II hover-wagon," Melody said, lifting a
large package into the back compartment. "I know several
jokes about this model."

"It's big enough for us all to camp in," Zara said, ignoring Melody.

"Yes, if it doesn't break down on the way." Belle stared at the clunky hover-wagon. With its landing gear lowered, and its side panels removed, it looked like a cross between an old camper in a scrapyard, and an ancient wagon from her history texts. She didn't want to know what jokes Melody could tell about it. "Will it get off the ground?"

"With Loki's help, it will," Yun said.

Belle walked around to the front of the wagon. There, harnessed to the wagon was the most enormous creature she'd ever seen.

"It's a horsel," Zara said, smacking her hands on her trousers. "A horse and camel hybrid. They can go for days without water and can outrun a dust storm, or so they say."

Belle stood back from the animal. Loki was twice the size of an Earth horse. He stared at her with his gentle, brown eyes. Belle took a step closer. She reached out her hand and stroked his nose. It was soft, warm and fuzzy.

"Hi there," she said timidly. She hadn't had much exposure to real animals. But from her virtual games, she knew they liked to be stroked and talked to.

Loki lowered his head and huffed, flaring his nostrils. Belle jumped back.

Yun laughed. "He's just saying hello."

Belle decided she would get to know Loki later. She helped her parents load supplies into the wagon instead.

When everything was packed, Belle sat in one of the seats in the back of the wagon. Melody strapped her in, and then did the same for herself. Yun and Zara sat at the front, on a bench seat that had the steering controls.

While Zara programmed the guidance system, Yun charged up the engine and retracted the landing gear. The wagon rose several metres in the air. Then pointing Loki west, the Song family left the town of Darwin behind them.

With Loki's size and the gravity difference, they travelled at a surprising speed. Most of the time, if Loki kept his pace steady, the wagon moved smoothly. Unfortunately, Loki was not always steady. The old wagon often leaned left and right as the horsel avoided rocks or stumbled over potholes.

From where Belle sat, her parents looked tiny compared to the giant creature they were guiding. Even with shoulder straps holding them in their seats, they still gripped the bench with all their might. As Loki tried to find his stride, the Song family was bounced and

jostled about. Belle hung on to Melody until her fingers were sore. Nobody spoke or moved as they left the outer limits of Darwin.

As they travelled west towards Sun City, where their farm was, they passed open field after open field.

"These are some of the earliest colonized farms," Melody explained. "Many of them grow versions of Earth crops that require the least amount of water."

Once past the farms, the land around them alternated between yellow grasslands and dusty desert-like plains. After a while, Loki picked up speed, which stabilized the wagon. The wind began to blow stronger. It was a refreshing change from the stifling heat of the town.

Melody turned up her volume so that Belle could hear her over the wind whistling past them. "Terraforming has made this land usable, but there are not enough farmers signing up for land. A lot of people prefer to work in asteroid mining."

Melody pointed out geological formations as they went along. Meanwhile, Belle fought the growling in her stomach. Soon she decided to unstrap herself and stood up. It was easier to balance now.

"I'm hungry," she said. "I'm going to get snacks."

"I should do that for you," Melody said.

"No, that's okay. I need to move around." Belle held onto the android's shoulders as she squinted at the scene around them. Everything was a blur because of how fast Loki was going. Belle held her breath in amazement.

"Please be careful," warned Melody.

Belle climbed over some packages stacked up in front of her. She found her pack and pulled out the snack bars she'd brought with her from Earth. She also grabbed a scarf for herself and one for Melody. The wind was getting chillier with each passing kilometre. Then she carefully climbed back over the packages, holding the scarves in one hand and her precious snacks in the other.

But just as she reached the edge of her seat, Loki faltered and the wagon tilted. Belle was jolted off her feet for a second. Shoving the snack bars between her teeth, she reached for Melody's outstretched hand. But then the wagon dipped suddenly, jolting Belle again. She yelled out, and her snack bars fell out of her mouth. Without thinking, she reached out to snatch them back. But the wagon jerked a third time, and Belle lost her balance.

She fell through the opening in the side of the wagon and floated in the air for the longest second of her life.

Then, *THUMP!* Her backside hit the ground and she went rolling – over and over. She didn't notice any pain at first. She only wanted to stop rolling. She couldn't even scream because air was forced out of her lungs with each bump.

In the distance, she heard Melody's voice calling for the wagon to stop. More yelling followed, then she heard the pounding of hooves and a deep grunting-neighing sound. She finally stopped rolling, but she couldn't move. She inhaled dirt, which made her cough . . . causing her to inhale even more dirt. Her lungs ached, and her heart raced. Tears blinded her. She soon felt every pebble under her stabbing at her face and bare arms. Slowly, her scraped skin started to burn. Then her bones began to throb. She found her breath and let out a terrible scream.

Mars Day 3, Summer, 2335, evening
Somewhere on the plains outside of Darwin

I fell out of the hover-wagon! Stars, did it hurt! Mum and Dad patched me up with the med-kit we had just bought. Nothing broken, according to the handheld scanner. Could've fooled me. Ooh, the pain! Now my arms and legs are blue and green, and all scratched up. It's hard to hold this pencil. Mum said it was a miracle I didn't hit my head. Dad didn't say a word the whole time. Mum put some weird cream on my wounds. She said it was Martian medicine. It smells strange — like flowers that have died in a vase. At least I don't hurt so much now...

Ugh... the smell of the cream just made me throw up. And now, even the air outside smells awful — like damp washing. We got caught in a dust storm, so we've stopped for the night to rest. We parked our wagon in front of a small cave. Loki gets to sleep in there while we camp in our wagon. Outside, it sounds as if a million cows are on a stampede, but it's only the wind and the sand. I hope we don't get trapped in here like we used to back at home during snowstorms.

This is NOT a great way to start a new life!

CHAPTER FOUR
∶THE SHACK∶

The dust storm lasted all night, but when morning came, everything was very quiet. So quiet, that for a moment Belle thought she had lost her hearing. Looking out of the wagon window, she saw that the land was a yellowish brown, as if some giant had laid its blanket on the ground. Everything as far as she could see was covered in sand-coloured dust.

Belle's body ached and her skin itched. She tried to get up, but it hurt too much to move.

"You're going to stay put for the rest of the journey," her mum insisted.

Belle stared at the wagon ceiling while her family cleaned off the wagon and fed and harnessed Loki. She felt the wagon rise and then jerk forwards as they began to move again. Yun had replaced the wagon's side panels, and Belle wished she could see more than the small clouds passing by through the small windows. Instead, for the next few hours she listened to Melody tell the most awful jokes about horses and camels.

The journey to their farm took them through the southernmost area of Olympia. It was cooler here than in Darwin, so Zara insisted that Belle wrap herself in several blankets.

Melody showed Belle various holo-maps of the region. She told Belle how the seasons on Mars lasted much longer than on Earth. Right now they were in the middle of the summer season, which was why it was so hot. Later on, they played several games of 3D chess. Finally, Belle grew tired and drifted off to sleep.

● ● ● ●

She was woken by Loki's grunting. The wagon had stopped, and Belle was all alone inside. She couldn't hear or see either of her parents. Even Melody was gone. Belle pushed herself up with her elbows and winced.

"Mum! Dad!" she cried, but no one answered her. She took several deep breaths and called out again. "Melody!"

"We're here," Zara said, poking her head in through the back door. "We're at our farm." She didn't sound very excited.

"What's wrong?" Belle asked, trying to get onto her feet.

"Wait for Melody to come and help you," Zara said. She bit her lower lip. "It's not quite what we were expecting."

Belle felt a tinge of pleasure when she heard that. *Maybe now we can finally go home*, she thought as Melody helped her out of the wagon.

It was the middle of the night, and the air was cold. The only light came from the millions of stars above and one of Mars' moons, Phobos. Melody's wide-beamed headlamp lit up the ground immediately in front of them. Belle shivered and rubbed her arms. After the heat of the cities, she wasn't used to how cool it was at night. The ground beneath her feet was covered in pebbles, and they crunched with each step. In the distance, Belle saw shapes – trees, perhaps. And there were two barn-like buildings, all dark grey and shadowy.

Right in front of Belle was a smaller building. Melody shone her light in that direction. When the beam landed on their new home, Belle groaned. The house was a run-down shack. The roof was crooked and leaned to one side. Several window shutters were bent out of place, and one hung unsteadily on a hinge. The place looked like it hadn't been lived in for a hundred years.

Yun had settled Loki in the smaller barn just beyond the house and was returning to unload the wagon. He flashed Belle a smile that looked like a grimace.

"It'll look better in the morning," he said. He was trying so hard to make her believe they had made the right decision.

"I'm sure it will," she said. She didn't say what she really felt – that her dad had made a big mistake by dragging them out here.

"Maybe we should spend the night in the wagon," Zara suggested. "We'll unpack in the morning."

That night, it took Belle a long time to fall asleep. She wondered just how much worse things had to get before her parents would finally give up.

● ● ● ●

When she woke up again, the sunlight was streaming through the open window beside her. She rubbed her eyes and sat up, surprised that her body didn't hurt as much anymore. That horrid-smelling Martian medicine really worked after all.

Belle got out her diary and began to write down her thoughts about their new home. As she wrote, she heard voices outside. But the voices didn't belong to her parents.

Peering out of the wagon's window, she saw a woman and a boy talking to Yun and Zara. The woman was taller than her dad. Her long, copper coloured hair was tied in a ponytail that fell to her thighs. She also had rough, purplish skin. The boy beside her had similar purple skin as well.

Aliens!

Mars Day 5, Summer, 2335, morning

The sunlight is so bright it woke me up. All is quiet inside the wagon. Perfect for diary writing. I don't ache so much anymore. It doesn't even hurt to write. Not like last night. Ow! I never want to feel that kind of pain again.

My parents and Melody must be moving things into our new home — which is awful! Our "homestead" (as Dad calls it) is old and rundown. I don't think anyone has lived here in years. Mum doesn't like it either, but she won't say anything to Dad. Still, I can tell she feels like I do. Dad, I'm not sure . . . I don't think he's as excited as he appears. I think they secretly wish their engineering jobs with BAMCorp had worked out.

I don't believe it — my parents are talking to two aliens!

CHAPTER FIVE
:UNEXPECTED:
GUESTS

Belle had never met an alien – they weren't allowed to visit Earth. But she'd heard there were many aliens on the off-world colonies, such as Lunar Colony, and here on Mars. And here were two aliens, talking to her parents!

Belle's mind was full of questions as she walked towards the visitors. She wondered what planet they were from and how long their journey to Mars was. She wanted to know everything about them.

But the questions stuck in her throat. She was an alien too, in a way. True, most Martians were human, but Belle was born and raised on Earth. That made her as much an alien here as the purple people now laughing with her parents like old friends. How would *she* feel if they shot question after question at her on their very first meeting? She decided the questions could wait.

"I'm so sorry," she heard the lady say. "We really had no idea this farm was taken. We often drop by for a rest when we're out on our walks. But we're so happy you're here now. This farm has badly needed a *korDar* – a family."

"We're just so thrilled to meet a neighbour," Zara replied. She looked back at the shack. "Even though we're not quite ready to be good hosts."

Yun waved Belle over. "This is our daughter, Isabelle."

"It's *Belle!*" she corrected. She hated it when her parents used her full name. It sounded so formal.

The woman nudged the boy. He was about Belle's age, and looked very much like a human. But when Belle looked more closely, she saw that he had arm and neck ridges like his mother. His skin was a lighter colour purple though. Belle tried not to stare.

"I'm Lucas," he mumbled, looking at his feet.

What an odd boy!

"And I'm Myra Walker," his mother said. Her purple skin shone in the sunlight, highlighting flecks of gold on her ridges and the sides of her face. She shook Belle's hand with such warmth, Belle liked her instantly.

"You're so shiny," Belle blurted, wide-eyed and staring. *Oh dear, did she just say that out loud?*

"Belle!" Both her parents gasped in unison.

"That's not very polite," Zara chided. "Please apologize."

"I'm sorry." Belle could feel her face burning with embarrassment.

Lucas scowled at her, but Myra laughed. "It's okay," she said. "You've probably never met a Sulux before."

"Sulux?"

"People from Suluxa," Lucas said. He looked annoyed at having to explain. Belle felt like such an idiot.

"My family has lived on Mars for a hundred cycles," Myra said. "I'm actually half Sulux and half human. Lucas is one-quarter Sulux. But my ancestors are from the planet Suluxa. It's the fifth planet in a nearby binary system. That means it has two suns. They arrived here around the same time Terrans colonized Mars."

"It was Sulux technology that helped terraform Mars." Lucas said.

"What's a cycle?" Belle asked.

Lucas rolled his eyes. "You don't know? A cycle is one revolution around the Sun. Duh."

"Now it's your turn to apologize," Myra said to her son. Then to Belle, she added, "A hundred cycles on Mars is about 190 Earth years."

"Oh, I didn't know," Belle said, staring at her feet. She hated sounding like a fool.

Myra put her hand on Belle's shoulder. "Don't worry, child," she said. "You'll soon get used to your new life on Mars. This world is so rich and full of new discoveries."

"Like Water Raiders!" Lucas' eyes lit up.

"What are those?" Belle said. They didn't sound like fun.

Myra scowled and waved her son away. "Not something to worry about right now. My husband, Padraig, is back at our homestead. He can fill you in on that topic. We live just to the south-east of here. You probably passed our farm on your way here."

She pointed in the direction they'd come last night. Belle saw nothing but yellowed grassland and clusters of enormous trees stretching up to the sky.

"We couldn't see much on the way in; it was too dark. We relied completely on the guidance computer," Yun said, scratching his head. "Plus, I'm afraid our home doesn't look any more livable in the daylight than it did last night."

Myra laughed. It was a great sound – like a flock of happy birds twittering. "That's not your real house. We call it the front porch. It has no security. Anyone, like us, can just walk in. But come with me. Let me show you how we live on Mars."

The entire Song family let out a sigh of relief. Even Melody seemed to perk up as they followed Myra back towards the house. She led them into the shack. Inside, there was a single table and two chairs in the middle of a large and very dusty room. At the other end was another door. This one was heavier and more solid than the front door. To the side of the door was a small wooden flap. Myra lifted it, revealing a computer panel hidden behind it. She turned to Yun.

"Do you have your security key code?" she asked. "It should be on your ownership file."

Yun pulled out his datapad and pulled up the relevant page. He entered the endless string of numbers and letters into the computer panel. The panel lit up, flickered red several times, and finally settled on a bright green glow.

"Now, each of you stand here, one at a time," Myra said, gesturing to a spot in front of the computer panel. "Let the computer scan you so your house will recognize you."

"It's just like back home on Earth," Belle said.

"Mars isn't behind Earth in any way, you know," Lucas said sulkily. "In fact, we're definitely ahead in environmental tech and terraforming knowledge."

Myra shushed him.

"What?" Lucas looked up at his mum. "Terrans who are new to Mars always expect us to be backward. I was just explaining the truth."

Myra sighed and nodded.

"That's not what I meant," Belle spoke through gritted teeth as the computer took her image. She didn't really like this boy. Maybe he didn't like the idea of Terrans moving to Mars.

Once the scanning was complete, they each had to say their name and a few key words so the computer would recognize their voices. Finally, the computer displayed "Welcome Home, Song Family" on the entrance panel. Then the door clicked open.

Myra led them through the door and down a set of stairs. With each step, a light came on, illuminating their way. It was cold inside, and the air smelled stale. Then the sound of a fan told Belle that the heater had turned on. She could feel the air warming up as they reached the bottom of the stairs. Myra waved her hand in a wide circle.

"Welcome to your real home," she said. "It's a little dusty, but I think you'll agree it's quite pleasant. The building above is really just a false front, to make it seem more like a home on Earth. It's a human thing, I suppose."

They were greeted by a white-walled kitchen filled with equipment that, by Earth standards, was seriously old. There was a large fridge, a food hydrator and a microwave oven.

"All water taps are equipped with purifiers too," Myra said. "The house has all the modern conveniences you could ask for."

"I can learn to use these," Belle heard Zara whisper to Yun.

There was also a small dining table, a living area, three small bedrooms and two tiny bathrooms. One bathroom held a water shower, while the other was equipped with a sonic shower.

"Mars law prohibits more than one water shower per week," Melody informed everyone. "Water is even more precious on Mars than on Earth."

Myra and Lucas eyed Melody suspiciously, as she spoke. *They don't like her*, thought Belle. *I wonder why?*

"We can handle that." Yun sounded cheerful. "On Earth, we had very strict restrictions on water usage too."

Belle could tell his cheerfulness was fake. She knew he hated sonic showers. He always said it didn't feel like he was any cleaner just because some fancy vibrations removed surface dirt and old skin.

Belle leaned against a wall as she took in the idea of living underground. There were no windows. It felt like they would be living in a box. Then her hand rubbed against the wall behind her. It came to life – displaying the view of their homestead outside. She stared at the wall. It was just as if she were looking out of a window at the stone path that led to the shack above. Beyond that, she saw the yellowish-green pasture and the two barns. She even saw Loki's head peeking out of his stall.

"It's a viewscreen!" she gasped.

"Yeah. It's really cool." Lucas' eyes lit up. For a second, he actually smiled. "You can programme any of the walls to display what's outside in real time. Or you can see other locations on Mars, or Lunar Colony or even Earth."

"This way you don't feel so claustrophobic," Myra explained. "The weather on Mars makes it hard for us to live above ground most of the time."

"We Martians don't have a problem with living underground," Lucas added. "But I've noticed Terrans hate the idea."

"Only at first," Myra said. She nudged her son. "And in the non-winter months, it can be quite pleasant to spend the day *deng yav* – upstairs."

"When there are no dust storms," Lucas grumbled.

"Does it ever snow?" Belle guessed Lucas would laugh at her for asking, but she didn't care.

"Not often, and only in winter, which lasts one hundred and fifty sols," Myra said. "Winters here are often severe. We rarely leave the house, so it's important to stock up."

"Sols?"

Myra looked pleased to answer Belle's questions. "I see you're a curious person, Belle. That's a very good quality to have. A sol is one day on Mars. It is thirty-seven minutes longer than one Earth day."

Belle caught the smirk on Lucas' lips. She really didn't like him.

Sol 98/Summer, Cycle 105
(Myra said that's how to write the date
here on Mars.)

Myra Walker is so genuine and nice. Her son,
Lucas, is something else. I get the feeling he doesn't
like new people. I was hoping we wouldn't have to see
each other much after today, but stars, was I wrong!
 The Walkers are our closest neighbours. Before
they left today, Myra invited us to their home, so
Mum and Dad could learn about farming from her
husband. I'm quite relieved that someone will be
showing us what to do to survive.
 But then she dropped the bombshell! She said
that because we're about the same age, Lucas and I
will be in the same class. The parents thought that
was great news. Lucas didn't look too thrilled. I know
I wasn't either. Hopefully, the class will be big enough
that we won't have to talk much. Otherwise, I'll never
get away from this grumpy, sarcastic boy.

 PS — Things to remember:
 1 Mars cycle = 687 days = 1.9 Earth years
 My age on Mars = 12/1.9 = 6.32 Mars cycles
 8 sols = 1 week on Mars

CHAPTER SIX

VISITING THE NEIGHBOURS

"What a perfect day for a walk to our new neighbours," Zara said. It was a bright and sunny morning. Low, puffy clouds floated on a gentle breeze.

It made Belle feel homesick for Earth.

"Walk?" Belle looked around. "How far is it to the Walkers' farm? Why can't we take Loki and the wagon?" She couldn't tell where their own farm ended and the next one began.

"It's only a few kilometres. We'll take our time and explore a little," Yun said.

In the daylight, the Songs' farm looked a lot more pleasant. Large clumps of bushy trees dotted their property as far as the eye could see. Crossing in front of their farm gate was a dirt road that seemed to stretch on forever.

"This is Aonia Road. It links all farms in the area," Melody said, projecting a holo-map of the area. "It joins the route to Darwin to the south-east and runs to Sun City to the north-west."

Melody was always full of useful information like that. If nothing else, Belle could spend the day listening to Melody's fun facts about Mars. But then Yun told Melody that she had to stay behind and watch their house. The android shut the gate and headed back to their house. Belle huffed.

"You saw how Myra and Lucas reacted to her when they were here," Yun said. "The Robot Rebellion didn't happen on Mars, but news travels. They might not be comfortable with the idea of robots being part of the family."

Belle huffed again. The rebellion ended almost fifty years ago. Were people really still afraid of androids?

"You know," Zara said. "If we didn't have Melody, we might be terrified of androids too. Let's get to know our Martian friends first, before introducing her, okay?"

Belle didn't answer. Anybody could see that Melody was special. She wasn't going to try and take over the planet or anything. She was Belle's best friend.

"Myra told me that Sun City is where the marketplace is," Zara said, changing the subject. "You love markets, don't you, Belle?"

Belle shrugged. She knew her mum was trying to lift the mood. But Belle didn't want to like Mars, and she missed having Melody around. Her mum sighed quietly.

The road they walked along separated two distinct biomes. On one side was plot after plot of flat grassland. Some of it was fenced in by wooden posts with laser crossbeams in between. Yun pointed out where the Song farm ended and the Walkers' began. Belle was surprised at how big their land was and worried at the same time. What would they do with all of this land?

On the other side of the road was a lush green forest that seemed to go on forever. Tall trees rose high into the sky. At the top, they stretched out their branches like arms, touching their neighbours. Their leaves wove together to shadow the forest in almost complete darkness.

"Trees were vital for terraforming Mars," Yun said, looking back at Belle, who stared with curiosity at the forest. "Strips of forestland like this were planted to help purify the air, and to prepare the soil for eventual farming. A hundred cycles ago, much of our farmland was forest too."

"I thought that removing the forests on Earth was what helped to destroy the air," Belle said, remembering all she'd learned at home.

"You're right," Yun said. "That's why some forests on Mars will be permanent."

"Like this one?"

"I don't know. But I'm sure you could ask your new teacher when you start school."

Belle didn't want to think about school. She hated the idea of being the new kid. She dragged her feet along as she followed her parents. They were holding hands and chatting, far too happily for Belle.

The Walker farm was almost exactly like the Song farm, except for the unusual crops growing in the fields. Belle couldn't make out what they were. Behind the fields were the pens, where several animals grazed. Belle spotted three horsels that looked even bigger than Loki.

Next to them were a group of creatures that resembled sheep, but Belle couldn't be sure. A handful of huge alpacas grazed in another area near a giant barn. One of the alpacas saw the Songs coming and bounded over to greet them.

"Wow!" Yun cried. "I've never seen an animal jump that high."

The sight of this huge animal leaping high off the ground was so amusing, Belle forgot for a moment that she was in a bad mood. She laughed and ran over to the waiting alpaca. With each step, she pushed against the ground a little harder. The land beneath her felt like a trampoline. She soared higher and higher with each leap.

"Look at me!" she cried.

"It's the gravity difference." Yun laughed, leaping next to her.

Belle was breathless when she reached the fence. She'd been so busy missing Earth, that she didn't think how fun it might be to explore a different planet. She and Yun petted the alpaca for a while, before Zara called them over to the Walker house.

As the Songs walked up the driveway, they saw a small building similar to the one on their own farm.

The Walkers had obviously done theirs up to look more livable, but it still had a shack-like appearance. Belle wondered if that was on purpose. Maybe it was meant to act like camouflage. If so, who were they trying to fool?

Padraig Walker ran up to the house as soon as he saw the Songs. He was a funny man with curly gold hair and a sunburnt face. He waved and shook hands as if he couldn't be happier to meet another person.

"Call me Paddy," he said with a catchy laugh.

Myra and Lucas soon joined the group. Within seconds, the parents were all chatting like old friends. Belle and Lucas stood staring at each other in silence.

Myra and Paddy began showing the Song family around their farm.

"Alpacas are one of the few Terran animals that haven't struggled to adapt to life on Mars," Myra said, pointing out their herd. "Except that they seem to grow bigger with each generation."

"What's wrong with your sheep?" Belle said.

Lucas snorted.

"They're shoats," Myra said. "Hybrid sheep and goats. Scientists cloned the first shoats to adapt to Mars. Since then they've become a natural farm animal here. They're our own version of livestock. Aren't they cute?"

Belle didn't think so.

"So you only have twenty-four alpacas?" Yun asked as they passed the grazing animals. "How is that enough to survive?"

"The authorities are very serious about limiting livestock," Paddy said. "Mars' ecosystem is much more sensitive than Earth's. They outlawed cattle because the methane gas they produced damaged the atmosphere. Alpacas are the new cows."

"The large numbers of cattle on Earth helped to ruin its atmosphere." Lucas had his hands on his hips, and spoke as if he knew everything. Belle couldn't stand him.

"Now, Lucas," his dad warned. "You know we learned from the mistakes of the past. So now we have a better life here. Livestock numbers are purposely kept low. Only a few farms are allowed to have animals. You're lucky the De Sousa family retired. Otherwise, you wouldn't have received a livestock licence. We live mostly on turken fowl and shoat. Alpacas are farmed for their milk and wool. Their meat is a rare luxury."

Paddy pointed out the crops he was growing – millet, beans and a hybrid squash-courgette.

"These require less water than traditional crops. Water is our most treasured resource." Paddy led the

Songs to an area behind their house. "That's why we spend so much money and energy on securing our water tanks."

"Where is the tank?" Belle couldn't see anything but a large yard.

"You're standing on it," Paddy said proudly.

"So it's underground? Why do you keep the tank hidden?" Zara asked.

"Raiders," Lucas whispered with a wicked gleam in his eyes.

"Raiders are never funny," Myra scolded her son. "And I don't like you scaring our new friends."

Paddy crouched to the ground and lifted a patch of earth. Hidden underneath was a computer panel similar to the one that opened Belle's house door.

"Water Raiders," he said. "They often try to steal our water. They're organized and ruthless. That's why it's vital to secure our tanks like this. Replacing the water is expensive. It can destroy a farmer's livelihood."

Belle felt a shiver go through her body. "What do these Raiders look like?"

The Walkers shook their heads in unison.

"We don't need to think about that now," Paddy said, replacing the patch of earth covering the computer panel.

He put his arm around Yun. "Let me show you how you can secure yours."

Myra slipped her arm into Zara's. "No more unpleasant talk. Let me show you our barn." She put on a smile, one that Belle could tell was forced. As much as Belle wanted to hear more about Water Raiders, she went along with Myra. Lucas dragged his feet behind her.

The barn was a high-ceilinged, double-storey building. It smelled like rotting vegetables. The floor was covered with brown and tan wood shavings. On the ground level were pens that held the funniest two-legged creatures Belle had ever seen.

"What are they?" She crouched down to look through the netting to get a better look. They had tails like turkeys. Their faces were a strange mix of turkeys and chickens – and they stank.

"You've never seen a turken?" Lucas said.

"They're a hybrid fowl," Myra said. "We're allowed to have more of these than alpacas, because they're smaller and don't pollute as much. They smell unpleasant, but they're quite delicious."

Belle whipped around with her eyes wide. "You actually *eat* these?"

Myra laughed her bird laugh again. "That's the farming life. We have to eat what we grow. So we eat some of the turkens, and we sell others at the markets. They also provide us with eggs, which we sell too. Their feathers are made into household items, and we grind up their bones into feed for our mealworms. We don't waste a thing."

She led Belle and Zara to the second level of the barn. It was clean up here and had no smell. There were long counters that held transparent tanks, each containing thousands of wriggling worms. Above each tank, a warming light lit the worms, giving them a bluish tinge. Belle felt her skin crawl. She wanted to run outside, fast.

"Mealworms are the staple food of Mars," Myra said. "They're cheap to grow and very nutritious." She picked up a worm and showed it to Belle, who jumped back a few steps. "They can be ground into flour, fried or baked. They're very useful and produce no pollution at all."

"They're environmentally friendly," Lucas said, appearing out of nowhere. He carried a box with him.

As Myra put the worm back, Belle noticed her hands.

"You have six fingers?" Belle asked in amazement.

Myra smiled. "A blessing of the Sulux."

As they left the barn, Lucas handed Belle the box he was carrying. Belle heard scratching sounds coming from

within. She lifted the lid and gasped. Four tiny chicks stared at her. They smelled like old socks. Belle wasn't sure what to make of them.

"These are for you, Belle," Myra said with a big smile. "You can learn a lot when caring for other living creatures. Treat them with respect, and they will serve you well."

"Thank you," Belle said, trying not to gag at the chicks' smell. Her mum gave her a stern look, so she stuck a finger in the box, pretending to stroke them. She couldn't wait to get home and dump them in the barn. She had no intention of taking care of them. Her mum could do that.

"I feel overwhelmed," Zara said. "There's so much to learn about this life."

Myra put her hand on Zara's shoulder. "That's what neighbours are for. We're all here to help each other."

Walking back to the house, Belle held the box at arm's length, faking excitement about her new "pets". Lucas walked beside her, sneering the whole time.

"What?" Belle said, as he led them into their house.

"I didn't say anything," he said.

Belle felt he was mocking her. He probably thought she'd fail at farming life. She was afraid he might be right.

I admit it. There are some things that I like about Mars. On a nice day like today, it feels a lot like Earth. I like the gravity too, because I can jump pretty high. My highest leap today was so high I could almost have landed on Dad's shoulders.

But I don't like it enough to want to stay here forever. I put those turkens into the big barn. They scratched me with their sharp claws. I have the marks to prove it. One of them even pecked me. That really hurt! They're not the sweet creatures Mum seems to think they are. They're evil and they hate me — just like Lucas.

I still can't believe I have to see him at school next week. I persuaded Mum to walk there with me on the first day, as it will be a new school on a whole new planet and everything. As for walking with Lucas after that? Maybe I'll suddenly take up cross-country running — or cross-country leaping — so he won't want to keep up with me, and I'll be rid of him.

CHAPTER SEVEN
:MELTDOWN:

Life as a farmer was hard.

The turken chicks stank up the barn. They pooped everywhere and pecked at Belle whenever she tried to touch them. They scared her.

She made Melody help her clean the pen, because the android didn't mind being pecked. But when her parents found out they took Melody away to help Yun with the water tank repairs.

"Myra gave you those chicks to learn how to care for other living creatures," Zara said. "How will you learn if Melody does all the work?"

So every morning, Belle was left alone with her killer chicks. In the afternoons there were farm chores, most of which she did by herself too. She tended her mum's vegetable patch and helped her dad put up fence posts around the pens. He made it her job to see that every fence post was properly placed. She also had to check the criss-crossing laser beams between the posts to make sure they functioned correctly. Then she cleaned the house and studied how to care for the new farm animals that her parents had applied for. But the worst chore of all had to be mucking out Loki's stall every day. Belle couldn't believe how much of a mess a horsel could make. After three days of this, she was tired and bored.

On the fourth day, her parents received their permits to grow crops and keep livestock.

"There's such a shortage of farmers," Yun said. "The authorities are practically giving these permits out as you land in Olympia."

A truck arrived two days later. It carried several bags of seed, twenty-four alpacas, thirty-six shoats and a small flock of turken.

"I didn't think the animals would arrive this quickly," Zara said, examining the alpacas.

Belle approached a shoat. It rammed her legs with its hard head. From a distance these animals were almost cute. But up close, they could be scary.

For the next week, Belle rose with the sun and worked all day helping her parents around the farm. They fed and watered the animals twice a day. There was now even more mucking of pens and stalls for Belle to do. Yun programmed and reprogrammed the laser fences to the right intensity.

"We don't want to fry these poor animals before we learn how to care for them, do we?" Yun said. He laughed, ignoring Belle's sulky face.

Belle didn't think any of this was funny. Each day she longed to go back to Earth, to city life, and to going out to the holo-cinema with her friends. But her parents wouldn't listen. They were too busy being happy about "going back to their roots" and "being the backbone of a new civilization". Someone forgot to tell them that Mars was not a new civilization – it was more than a hundred cycles old.

Then there was the food. Myra was wrong when she said mealworms were delicious. They were tough and chewy. Zara ground them into flour and made bread.

Belle barely nibbled at it. She kept seeing the disgusting worm wriggling in Myra's six-fingered hand. It was a good thing the Walkers had given them some meat and eggs or Belle would've starved.

At dinner time on the night before school, Belle was in a foul mood. She didn't want to start school. She'd had enough of her chicks, and she'd definitely had enough of being a farmer. Yun was telling stories about his trip into Sun City for supplies. Zara suggested names for their alpacas. But Belle felt more and more miserable. Her parents would never want to leave. She'd never see Earth again. She stared at the food on her plate, pushing the beans around with her fork.

"Aren't you eating?" Zara asked. Yun stopped talking and looked at Belle as if he hadn't noticed her lack of appetite until that moment.

"Not hungry," murmured Belle.

"Well, you need to keep up your energy," Yun said. "You've got school tomorrow. Now, eat."

"No." Belle smacked her fork onto her plate.

"Isabelle Song . . ." her mum warned.

"*What?*" Belle dared to glare at her mum, but only for a second.

"What has got into you?" Yun asked. "You were quite happy helping me with the animals today."

"I'm never happy," Belle said. "Not anymore."

"Oh dear," Yun said, leaning back in his chair. "Is this what we have to look forward to when you're a teenager?"

"*Really*, Yun?" Zara said.

Belle jumped out of her seat. "Dad! Stop it! Why can't you just listen to me?"

"Then tell us, what's wrong?" Zara asked.

"Nothing!" Belle got louder with each sentence. "You two just don't get it. You're acting like you've been farmers your whole lives, when you know nothing! In the meantime, I have no friends and no life! I hate Mars. I want to go home!"

"I understand. It's been a big change for all of us," Yun said. "But I bet you'll make new friends when you go to school tomorrow."

"Not if they're anything like Lucas Walker. All he does is laugh at me." Belle shoved her plate off the table, spilling food and making a loud clang that echoed through their house. "He was right about one thing though – I hate living underground!"

She stormed up the stairs and knocked over a chair in the shack. She stomped hard on the front step, putting a hole into the wood. Cursing it, she ran.

And ran.

The sun lingered on the horizon, lighting the sky
in blue first, blending upwards into a fiery red-orange.
Startled birds, searching for scraps, took flight, cawing
noisily as they rose into the chilly evening air.

Belle's face and lungs stung as the cold whipped by her.
She ran all the way to a big cluster of trees at the furthest
end of their farm. She leaned against a wide trunk, rubbing
the stickiness of dried tears off her cheeks.

She slid down to the ground and lay her head against
the rough tree bark, listening to her own breath and the
silence around her. Earth didn't have this kind of silence.
It was frightening, but also sort of comforting. Slowly, she
drifted off, dreaming of her home on Earth, and her old
friends, whose faces faded away one by one.

The sudden sound of grass rustling woke her.

"Who's there?" she called. The familiar squeak of
her android's joints told her she was safe. "How did you
find me?"

"I followed you," Melody said. "I was giving you some
space, as humans like to say."

"Thanks," Belle said. It was nice to know that at least
Melody understood her.

"I advise you to return to the house now. It is dark and
getting very cold."

Belle rose to her feet and stretched. "I'm not ready to go back yet."

"How do trees get on the internet?" Melody asked.

"What? I don't know. What do you mean?"

"They simply log on," Melody replied, waiting for Belle to laugh at her joke.

Belle shook her head. "You're going to have to work on your timing, Melody."

She looked up at the thick, low branches above her. They stretched outwards like giant arms. "Let's climb."

Belle reached up and swung one leg over the first limb, and then the next.

"You should not go any higher," Melody said, when Belle had climbed up four thick limbs.

Melody hovered up and landed on the tree next to Belle. The limb was wide enough to hold them both. They sat there in silence. As they looked out over the Song farm, the sun sank below the horizon. The sky was filled with shades of red, orange and purple. It was a spectacular sunset.

"It is a very pleasant farm," Melody said. "And located in an ideal spot."

"You don't approve of my outburst," Belle stated.

"It has only been two weeks," Melody replied. "You begin a new chapter tomorrow. You should give this life a chance."

Belle was about to tell Melody she sounded a lot like her mum, when she heard something.

"What was that?" It was a sound she'd never heard before.

They sat very still and listened. Nothing happened at first. Then, there it was.

"It sounds like a howl," Melody said.

"Shh!" Belle put her finger to her lips.

There was definitely a howling sound in the distance. Then something else howled back. Belle removed a pair of binoculars from Melody's central storage space. She focused them on the direction of the howls. But even with night vision activated, she couldn't see anything.

"It's getting closer," Belle said in a loud whisper. "Are you carrying any of my Petripuffs?" Belle had created the small, handheld defensive weapons as a science project the year before. They could paralyse an enemy long enough to let someone escape.

"Your father forbade them on the journey here," Melody said. "He said they were too dangerous to carry."

"Really? Too dangerous for an alien planet, with strange alien animals lurking in the darkness?" Belle tried to swallow her anger. She had to focus on those howls.

"We should return home," Melody said.

Belle wrapped her arms around Melody's neck. The android hovered down to the ground in seconds. Melody activated her light beam and guided Belle home. With each kilometre, more howls seemed to join in – each time sounding closer.

Belle's heart was pounding when she dashed inside the shack. She slammed the flimsy door behind them.

"What *was* that?" she panted.

"According to my archives, that was the night call of wolves," Melody responded.

The door to their underground home slid open. Her parents came rushing out.

"We were so worried!" Zara pulled Belle into a hug.

"You shouldn't be outside after dark," Yun said.

"Did you hear them?" Belle asked.

"Hear what?"

"Wolves!"

They stood very still for a long while, listening. There was nothing more than the occasional caw of an unknown bird outside.

Yun sighed. "There are no wolves on Mars. People here never cloned any predators, unless you count dogs. And they're tame."

"But I heard them!" Belle exclaimed. Her anger came flooding back.

"You have an active imagination, Belle," Yun said. Then he insisted that Belle go straight to bed. "You don't want to turn up on your first day of school exhausted and grumpy."

Sol 114/Summer, Cycle 105

Those were wolves I heard. I don't care that my parents don't believe me. I can't imagine hearing something that I've never heard before in my life! Whatever. I've got to start making more Petripuffs to protect myself. I've given Melody a list of ingredients to buy. I hope Dad doesn't notice my pocket money shrinking.

I'm not looking forward to school tomorrow. Martian kids go to school from Spring to Autumn because winters are too cold. Thank the stars we only go twice a week. The rest of our school work is done at home.

I'm sure I'll have a lot more to write about school — just don't expect it to be good.

CHAPTER EIGHT
AN UNUSUAL NEW FRIEND

The next morning was cold and misty when Belle crawled out of bed. She'd barely slept. She kept waiting for more wolves to howl to prove to her parents that she hadn't imagined it. But they never howled again, not once.

At breakfast, Belle wasn't in a good mood. She was angry with her parents for thinking she'd made up the wolf stuff. But she knew that arguing wouldn't solve anything. So she decided that she just wouldn't talk at all.

Zara and Belle left the house early, strolling through the fields and cutting across the back of their farm. They headed north and walked along a dirt path through another farm, and then another.

"I can't see Lucas," Zara said, breaking the silence.

Belle grunted.

"I wonder who lives here? It would be nice to get to know more neighbours, don't you think?"

Belle bent down to pull a stone out of her shoe. They walked on for a while longer.

"There!" Zara pointed ahead. "That's the school."

The low, box-like building stood alone in a vast empty area of grass and dust. It had smooth grey walls and barely any windows. Belle couldn't see a playground or a playing field anywhere. It was the saddest looking school grounds she'd ever seen.

Only when she squinted could she see the outline of a town beyond the building. She saw more low, boxy buildings with flapping canopies shading the alleyways between them.

That must be Sun City, Belle thought. The school was just outside the town.

Zara stopped and turned to Belle. "Okay, I understand that you're angry," she huffed. "But nothing ever got solved by sulking. If you want to be heard, you have to speak up."

Belle kicked at some stones at her feet.

"I know you're unhappy about moving here," Zara said, more gently. "But what did you expect us to do? We have no jobs with BAMCorp. And we can't exactly force them to give us work, can we?"

"That's not it," Belle mumbled.

"So you hate being a farmer." Zara threw her hands up. "What would you like us to do instead? I'm open to any ideas or suggestions."

Belle shrugged.

Zara sighed. "Well, when you think of something, let me know." She pointed to the building. "Do you think you could try to be polite to your teacher, at least?"

Belle gave her half a nod, and they walked on towards the school.

Sun City School occupied a corner of the grey block building. The building also housed a medical clinic, a library and the community centre. The school had children from nursery all the way to the end of secondary school. Children from all the farms in the area came here for their education.

"Your class is in room number one," the headmistress, Ms Yuko, said. She seemed nice, though Belle thought she smiled too much. "Please say your goodbyes now."

"Have a good day," Zara said. She opened her arms and Belle gave her a long hug that said "goodbye" and "I'm sorry" at the same time.

Ms Yuko walked Belle down the long, narrow corridor. There were three doors on each side, each slightly open. Belle looked back to watch her mum leave the building. She missed her already. Then someone tapped her on the shoulder.

Belle turned around, and her mouth fell open. Here was a girl (at least, Belle *thought* it was a girl) who was definitely not human. Her shoulder-length black hair looked like it was made of plastic. She had a high, ridged forehead, where her nostrils were. Her two large eyes seemed to glow grey and yellow. And her lips were a bright red, which made her smile surprisingly pretty. She lowered her head when Belle looked at her, and made a gesture with her hands, weaving them around like a dance.

"*Gyrvel* – Welcome. I'm your buddy for the day," she said, in a soft voice. "My name is Ta'al."

"Ta'al will show you around until you are comfortable," Ms Yuko said. "Have a productive day."

She disappeared back into her office.

"Are you Sulux?" Belle asked as Ta'al led her down the corridor.

"Oh no!" Ta'al said. "I'm Nabian. The Sulux don't really like –"

Before she could finish her sentence, someone ran past them, shoving Ta'al against the wall. Before he disappeared into the last room on the left, he turned back to look. It was Lucas Walker. He had a strange expression on his face as he looked at Ta'al and then at Belle.

"Hey!" Belle said. "Watch where you're going."

Ta'al smoothed down her long tunic and continued to lead Belle to the room Lucas had just entered.

"Are you all right?" Belle asked. "That wasn't nice of him."

"It was just *ivusyxd* – an accident," Ta'al said. "This corridor is very narrow."

Belle wasn't so sure of that.

Ta'al introduced Belle to their teacher. She was a tall, dark-haired human with green-blue eyes ringed by a circle of red.

"Good morning, I'm Ms Polley," she said. "Welcome to our class."

The classroom was a lot smaller than at Belle's old school. There was one large table for four pupils in the middle of the room. Four other small desks were scattered about the room. A holo-screen computer lay in front of every seat. Screens along the walls alternated posters for all the different ages of students that occupied this room.

Lucas, two boys and a girl sat around the large table. They were all human, except for Lucas. They were very tall for twelve-year-olds, which made Belle feel very small. They also had red ringed irises, just like their teacher. Was this a trait of Martian-born people?

"You will be our sixth pupil," Ms Polley said. "A nice even number."

A bell rang from somewhere outside. Ms Polley clapped her hands, and everyone turned to look at her.

"This is Isabelle, our latest addition," she said. She dragged two individual desks together and added, "You and Ta'al will be table buddies this term. I'll rotate you all next term."

Lucas and his table friends moaned. They stuck two fingers on their foreheads in some kind of secret signal. Ta'al looked away and took her seat. Belle glared at Lucas.

The lessons that day focused mostly on agricultural topics. Belle learned about the latest methods for growing meat in a lab and the needs of cross-bred animals. The class also discussed advancements in plant modification and the advantages of micro-algae. She wondered when they'd be learning maths, or her favourite subject – space science.

Through most of the lessons, Ta'al was silent. As the other pupils raised their hands and asked questions or gave comments, Ta'al seemed content to sit quietly and listen. She only spoke when Belle asked her questions. Even the teacher left her alone.

At lunchtime, Ta'al led Belle to a small canteen shared by all the classes. They sat at their designated class table. Belle met Trina, the other girl in their class, who seemed nice. Pavish, Brill and Lucas made up the rest of their table. They all spoke to Belle, asking her questions about her family and where she came from. Lucas even managed to ask her about the games she played. But no one spoke to Ta'al. It made Belle uncomfortable.

After lunch, the others invited Belle to join them outside. The weather was nice enough to be outside, and Martians took every chance they could to get some sunshine. They played a disc throwing game that Belle found too hard to keep up with. The Martian-born humans were taller and faster than her. She did her best but wasn't very good at the game. After watching for a few minutes, she wandered off by herself.

She spotted Ta'al sitting next to a tall tree stump. All its branches had been sawed off.

Belle sat down beside her. "Hi Ta'al. Why are you sitting by yourself? Don't you like the games we're playing?" she asked.

Ta'al closed the book on her datapad and looked over at the others.

"I prefer to read," she said.

"I do too," Belle said with a big smile. She liked Ta'al, and she hoped they could be friends. "Tell me about your book."

Ta'al seemed happy to talk about the story she was reading. Belle told her about her own favourite books. Before long, the two girls were laughing like old friends. When the bell rang, it was time for lessons to resume.

"I have an exciting announcement," Ms Polley said as they took their places. "The schools of Olympia are having a science fair, and we've been invited to compete."

At the words "science fair" Belle perked up. This was her kind of thing.

"I'm going to pair you up with a classmate, and you'll come up with a project to work on," Ms Polley continued. "One winning pair from each class will be chosen to represent our school in Tharsis City, the Martian capital of Olympia, next summer."

Belle's mind was racing with ideas. She looked at Ta'al.

"I hope we can be partners," she whispered.

"*Teyqarro.*" Ta'al crossed her fingers.

"First, I'd like us to discuss what we've done in previous years," Ms Polley said.

Belle was too busy coming up with ideas for projects to listen to her classmates. Besides, no one asked Ta'al about her ideas, so Belle almost didn't care. The others were polite enough to Belle, but she didn't understand why they ignored her new friend. She really hoped that Ta'al could be her partner. Together, they would come up with something amazing. Belle was certain that the other kids would then want to be friends with them both.

"Isabelle," Ms Polley called. Belle looked at her, realizing that she hadn't heard anything the teacher had said. "Tell us what you've done before."

Belle sat up straight. She loved talking about her science projects. She was an expert. "Well, my latest invention was a defensive weapon that I call Petripuffs.

They're covered with gel and are shaped like a ball that fits in your hand. You throw them at an enemy. If the ball hits, the powdered ingredients inside puff out to paralyse the target for about a minute. This gives the thrower the time needed to get away to safety."

Everyone gaped at Belle. Ms Polley coughed into her hand.

"I see." She spoke slowly, as if Belle didn't understand English. "In Olympian towns, we try to confine our science projects to those with agricultural applications. Perhaps you may have grown a plant in varied environments? Or extracted the DNA of a fruit?"

"Of course," said Belle, puzzled by the way er teacher was speaking. "Back when I was in nursery."

"Hmm. I see." Ms Polley walked around her desk and sat down. "I suppose you are new to our planet, so I can't expect you to be aware of . . . our priorities." She looked down at her computer screen. Looking back up, she seemed to have come up with an idea. "Seeing as you live so close to Lucas, I think it would be best if you were paired with him. What do you say to that?"

The expression on her teacher's face told Belle that she'd better say it was a great idea. But inside, Belle was horrified.

"As neighbours, you should be able to work together easily." Ms Polley leaned back in her chair. "And Lucas can help guide you in how we do things."

Belle couldn't look at Lucas, or at Ta'al. This day had turned out as badly as she'd expected – just when things had begun to look more hopeful.

Sol 115/Summer, Cycle 105

All we learn at school is farm stuff. It's all
SO boring!

I met a really nice girl. Her name is Ta'al. She's
Nabian, a different alien race from Lucas and
Myra. The others in the class treat her like she's
weird, but I think she's pretty. And she's fun to
talk to. I think we could be best friends. I don't
understand why the others don't like her.

Our teacher is odd too. She wasn't impressed
by my Petripuffs. Why not? They won the science
fair last year.

I can't believe I've been partnered with Lucas
for the science fair. Even worse — the projects all
have to be related to FARMING!!! Ms Polley said
it's because we're from Sun City and farming is
our "primary industry", whatever that means.

Aaaaaaaggghhh! It makes me want to scream!
I really wanted to be partnered with Ta'al. She got
Brill, and looked as horrified as I was. Poor girl.

At least Lucas seemed pleased to be my
partner. He didn't stop talking all the way home.
I was too busy thinking about Ta'al to hear what
he said. We're meeting in the big barn tomorrow.
I hope he's ready to hear my ideas.

CHAPTER NINE

NIGHTMARE PROJECT

"I don't want to experiment with turken chicks!"
Belle stomped her foot at Lucas, as he put his tools down
on the barn floor. He had an entire wheelbarrow full of
mesh wiring, wooden stakes and aluminium panels.

"It's our best chance of winning the science fair," he
said. It was the day after being paired with Lucas, and
Belle felt that he wasn't listening to a word she'd said. She
had lots of great ideas, but he kept shaking his head.

"Turken are so important to the economy of Olympia. We'll definitely win if we can find a way to grow them bigger and faster, without artificial means."

He went on and on. Belle heard only one in three words. The chicks in her pen made so much noise, it made her squirm. She couldn't bear the thought of getting scratched again.

Lucas moved about the barn, setting up three separate pens. He hammered and cut, while Belle stood there and watched him. When he was finished, he opened his arms wide, like a game-show host. "Here's the future – Super Chicks!" he said with a big smile. "They're all natural and more nutritious than ever before." He looked like he was expecting Belle to applaud.

She didn't.

"I don't really like chicks," she said.

"You don't have to like them to win the science fair," he said. "Now let's look for some bugs to feed one set of chicks."

"Bugs? There are bugs on Mars too?"

Lucas gave her a funny look. "Duh. They came along in the earliest bags of seed from Earth. They've been here ever since."

Belle cringed and gave up trying to protest. It didn't matter what she wanted. Lucas had already decided everything. What was the point of being his partner? He was a one-man show. She watched him lift rocks and scratch beneath tree trunks until he'd found several insects. Her skin crawled each time he showed them to her.

On their way back to the barn, he grew quiet. Belle was about to finally tell him why she would rather do something else for their project. But then he turned and said, "You're not much of a partner, are you?"

Belle couldn't believe her ears.

"What? *You're* not much of a partner!" Her cheeks were burning.

"I did everything today." He crossed his arms. "Is this the way it's going to be for the whole project?"

"You didn't even ask me if I wanted to do this," Belle retorted.

"You're new here," Lucas responded defensively. "You don't know what sort of projects win. And I heard your parents say you've never been farmers before. I was trying to be helpful."

Belle didn't have a chance to defend herself. Lucas stormed back into the barn, refusing to look at her. He poured his insects into one of the pens and then placed two turken chicks inside. He was spreading the insects around with a stick when Belle marched up to him.

"You're not being fair," she said. "We're supposed to be partners, but you've made all the decisions."

He didn't say anything. He wasn't even paying attention to her. Belle gritted her teeth and grabbed him by one shoulder. She tried to swing him around, so he'd at least look at her. She had to make him listen because he was being so unfair.

But instead of swinging around, Lucas lost his balance and fell backwards into the nearest pen. The posts holding it up fell over, which knocked down a second pen, and then the third. This terrified the larger turkens, which squawked and flapped their wings. One bird hopped onto Lucas' chest as he lay on the ground, while another flew straight at Belle's face. She screamed and turned her back on it, which scared it even more. It flapped and squawked again, scratching Belle's arms and back. It landed on her shoulders and started pecking at her head. Belle ran around the barn, flailing her arms, trying to get the bird to leave her alone.

Finally, the turken let go of Belle and fell to the floor. It clucked angrily and went back to its original pen.

"Just look at what you did!" She turned on Lucas.

"What *I* did? *You* shoved *me*."

"I did not," Belle shouted. "You've been nothing but a big bully."

Lucas stared hard at Belle, and then turned away from her. He got down on his hands and knees and gathered up the escaping insects. He dumped them into a bucket near by and then started to pick up the fallen posts.

Seeing Lucas' response, Belle realized that maybe she had taken things too far. "Be careful not to cut yourself on those wires," she said softly.

"What do you care?" he snapped. "You didn't lift a finger to help me build this."

"I really didn't mean to ruin all your work." She could see now how her anger had caused all of this mess. "Let me help you fix it. Please?"

Lucas' glare softened. Belle could see by the look on his face that he was trying to decide if he could trust her again.

"Fine," he said at last. "But let's do it tomorrow. It's getting late, and I have to go home for dinner."

● ● ● ●

All through dinner, Belle kept thinking about her terrible behaviour. Lucas had actually been nice to her. He had done so much work for a project they would both get credit for, and she hadn't helped at all. On top of that, he was coming back to fix the damage she had caused.

"May I go back to the barn tonight?" she asked her parents. "I have some work to do on our science project."

Her parents beamed at her.

"I knew you'd like it here once you went to school and made friends," Yun said. "Would you like Melody to help you?"

Belle shook her head. "This is my responsibility. I should take care of it." She couldn't bring herself to confess that it was her mess to clean up. And the less her parents knew about her bad behaviour that day, the better.

Sol 110/Summer, Cycle 105, night

It took hours of work, but I fixed all the broken pens. It was hard putting the fencing panels together the right way, but I worked it out. I even put the chicks in their respective new pens. I barely got scratched this time. I think they still hate me, but I'm getting better at handling them.

I'll check on them again in the morning before Lucas comes. I hope the one I pushed off me isn't hurt too badly. Lucas would never forgive me for that. What a stressful day!

Oh shooting stars! I forgot to lock the barn door!

CHAPTER TEN
ᗰᗩᖇᗶᗩᑎ ᗪᗩᑎᱤᗴᖇ

Sneaking out of the house was hard when every movement alerted the home computer system. As soon as Belle's feet touched her bedroom floor, the lights came on. As she headed for the front door, every room she passed lit up. Luckily, her parents' door was shut tight.

"Where are you going?" Melody unlatched herself from her charging port and strolled over to her. "May I help you?"

Belle put her finger to her lips. She told Melody about the barn door. Melody insisted on coming with her. Together, they made their way out to the barn. The night air was freezing so Belle ran. Melody hovered along behind her. She stopped suddenly.

"Wait!" Melody said.

"What is it?"

Then Belle heard it. Something was making a shuffling sound inside the barn. There was a whimper and another sound she couldn't describe. She tiptoed to the barn door. It was open. Belle swallowed the lump in her throat.

"Something's inside," she whispered.

"Throw open the door when I say so," Melody said, as she positioned herself in front of Belle. "Now!"

Belle swung open the door. Melody turned on her light beam. Staring back at them were four shining eyes. And two sets of sharp, gleaming teeth!

Wolves!

There really were wolves here. Like the llamas, these were much bigger than wolves on Earth.

Belle froze. For the longest moment, the wolves stared at Melody and Belle. Belle stared back.

"Step to the side, very slowly," Melody said.

Belle obeyed, moving over to the side. As she did, she saw the entire picture. Around the wolves' mouths and at their feet was a pool of blood . . . and bloody feathers.

Her chicks!

"No!" Without thinking, Belle ran towards the pen.

"Stop!" yelled Melody.

Belle stopped. Her heart was racing, but not because she was afraid of the wolves. One of her chicks lay dead on the ground in front of her. And the pens were destroyed. Chicks were hiding everywhere in the barn, shivering and frozen in fear. Suddenly a fire seemed to light inside Belle's chest. She screamed at the wolves and waved her arms at them.

"How dare you! You ruined everything!"

One of the wolves tilted its head to the side, making it look almost tame. Then the other wolf took a step forward. Belle heard a low growl coming from its chest. Slowly, it bared its teeth at her.

Belle realized what was happening, and now she
was scared. She wished she had some Petripuffs with
her. But she hadn't been able to make any. She was still
waiting for the ingredients to be delivered.

Melody placed herself between Belle and the
wolves. Her lower cavity opened and a yellow and
white stick emerged. It looked like an oversized
two-pronged fork. Belle had never seen it before.

"What is that?" she asked, careful not to take her
eyes off the wolves for a second.

"Your father thought we would need a livestock
prod," Melody said. "This should scare them." She
activated the device, and it crackled a flash of electricity
into the air. Belle jumped. The wolves cowered.

Melody made a rumbling sound similar to the
wolf's growl. She moved closer to the animals. They
stepped back, lowering their heads.

"Shoo!" Melody shouted.

One wolf yelped, turned tail, and ran out of the
barn. The other one bared its teeth even more, and
snapped at the android. Melody took another step
closer and repeated her order, only louder. The wolf
lunged at her. Belle screamed just as the barn door

swung open wide. Her parents stood in the doorway, the light of the night sky making them look like shadows.

"Get out!" Yun shouted. He moved towards the wolf. The animal crouched low on all fours as it saw the sonic blaster Yun was carrying. Belle heard the hum of the blaster charging. Zara ran to Belle's side.

"What's Dad going to do?" Belle had never seen her dad with a weapon before.

"Hush," said her mum. Belle held on to her mother.

Yun fired a shot at the ground next to the wolf, and it yelped. Keeping its eyes on the blaster, the wolf slinked past Yun and ran away into the night.

Belle burst into tears. She couldn't tell if it was due to fear of the wolves, all of the damage done, or because of the dead chick.

"Wolves!" Zara said. "Oh my! They're huge!"

"You were right, Belle," Yun said. "Are you hurt?"

"You shouldn't have come out alone," Zara said. "This isn't Earth, child. You can't keep going outside after dark. It's dangerous at night."

In between her tears and catching her breath, Belle told her parents how Melody had protected her. "I didn't even know Melody had an electric prod."

"I bought one in Darwin, just in case," Yun said.

Belle hugged her android. "You saved my life."

"I was simply performing my primary function. You behave rather recklessly in dangerous situations."

Yun chuckled, rubbing his face. "It's a good thing I practised using this blaster today. I didn't want to kill the wolf, but this definitely helped to scare it away."

Belle was still shaking from the encounter. As she looked around, she became even more upset about the chick that had died. The others around the barn looked all right, but they were too scared to come out of their hiding places.

"Lucas will never forgive me now."

Yun put his arm around Belle. "I'm sure he'll understand when we explain what happened."

Belle wasn't so sure about that. It was her carelessness that let the wolves into the barn in the first place. Yun picked up the remains of the turken chick and together they buried it outside.

"I'm sorry we didn't believe you about the wolves," he said. "We haven't been listening to you much, have we?"

"I'm sorry too." Belle hugged her dad. "I know I haven't been very helpful either."

They went back to the barn and Belle looked at all the damage. She couldn't let Lucas see this. "I want to fix this before I go to bed," she said.

"If we work together, it'll get fixed faster," Zara said.

Belle again at the mess. It seemed hopeless. If they couldn't fix this, Lucas might never speak to her again.

Sol 111/Summer, Cycle 105, almost morning

It's almost morning but I can't sleep. I'm exhausted but my eyes won't stay shut. I keep seeing those scary wolves' huge yellow eyes staring at me through the dark. And the sound of Dad's sonic blaster firing — my heart still hasn't stopped racing!

We worked all night to fix the pens. Mum and Dad were actually pretty cool about it. They didn't shout or tell me off even once. The pens look OK now. I sort of miss that one chick that died. I can't stop seeing its bloody body. It was a nightmare. Dad said some nice things about it when we buried it. It made me cry, but I suppose it was a bit silly at the same time.

What I'm worried about most is Lucas. When I see him later, he'll be so mad. What if he doesn't want to be my partner anymore? How will I get to compete in the Science Fair? After the way I've behaved, maybe I don't deserve to. Serves me right.

CHAPTER ELEVEN

:HOME:
SWEET HOME

Lucas arrived a few hours later. He brought more supplies to fix the broken pens. Belle's stomach twisted painfully as she explained to him what had happened the night before. As he listened, his shoulders slumped and his face darkened. Belle was afraid to hear what he was going to say. This had been all her fault. She braced herself for an argument.

"*Iqnah!*" Lucas mumbled without translating the word. Belle didn't want to know what it meant. She waited for more. He dug his toe into the dirt. "Looks like we have a lot of work to do today."

"I'm really sorry," she squeaked.

"Sulux have a saying – *Veth yln*. It's sort of like 'That's life'. Life here on Mars can be unpredictable. You didn't know about the wolves. How could you?"

Belle swallowed. She couldn't tell him she had heard the wolves once before.

"Why aren't you cross with me? I ruined everything."

He looked at her. "You didn't do any of that on purpose, did you?"

"No, of course not," she responded.

"Well then, what's the point of being mad? It just wastes energy. And we need to use our energy to fix the project."

He headed for the barn. Belle held the door for him. She waited outside for a moment, holding her breath.

"It doesn't look so bad," he said. "You did a good job of fixing things up."

"My parents helped. So did Melody." The pens looked almost as if nothing had happened. Except for the missing chick.

"Melody?"

"She's my android," Belle said. "A Personal Home Helper, model 3X. She's great."

"I've seen it around, but I didn't know it was an intelligent robot. Aren't you afraid?" he asked.

"Firstly, 'it' is a 'she'. Secondly, why should I be afraid?" she replied.

He put his supplies down. "Because of the Robot Rebellion on Earth, and everything that happened back then."

"That's old news," Belle said. "And Melody is even older. She belonged to my grandmother. Her model type wasn't responsible for the fighting or the attempt to overthrow the authorities. Those rebel robots were highly advanced. Besides, they were all taken offline and dismantled. Melody is completely safe. She's been my friend since I was a baby."

He nodded. "Okay. If you say so."

Belle looked at him. She had to work him out. Why was he being so nice to her?

"You didn't like me at first." The words just tumbled out. "And honestly, I wasn't sure I liked you either."

Why did she say that? Now, he'd definitely be angry with her. Sometimes she didn't think before she spoke, and it offended people. But Lucas just looked at the chicks searching for food in their pens and smiled shyly.

"I'm not very good with meeting new people. My mum says I'm an 'introvert', whatever that is. There is no Sulux word for it."

Belle started to say that it meant that he was shy. But she bit her tongue instead. She didn't want to come across as too much of a know-it-all, not when they were just beginning to get along.

"Honestly, a lot of Terrans move here, thinking life will be easy. They like to call it the 'simple life'. It's an insult, really. Farming on Mars is no picnic. I see how hard my parents work. They love it, but it's not easy. So sometimes I get mad with Terrans. Although, I see that your family is serious about making a go of it."

He pulled out a bag of seed and threw a handful into the pen. The chicks rushed towards it.

"I understand," Belle said quietly. She threw a handful of seed into the second pen.

He shrugged, not looking away from the chicks. "So, I'm sorry for being so rude. You're not so bad, after all."

"Thanks," Belle said. "You're not so bad yourself." She paused. "Why don't you like Ta'al? She's not Terran."

Lucas exhaled loudly. Something in his body language told her that this was not something he wanted to talk about.

"We really should get to work," he said.

Belle nodded. She knew not to push him for an answer. They were becoming friends. She didn't want to ruin it now. She could wait until he was ready to talk.

For the rest of the day, Belle did everything she could to be helpful. She didn't complain about how wriggly the chicks were, and she went out to dig for insects when Lucas asked her to. She did her best to ask lots of questions. Some of them seemed pretty stupid, but Lucas didn't seem to mind answering them.

All in all, it was a really good day.

In the evening, Lucas' and Belle's parents came to check on their project.

"We're so proud of how much work you two have done," Yun said.

"You're bound to win at the fair," Paddy chuckled.

Paddy asked Belle to explain what they were doing and, surprisingly, she was able to answer some of his questions. Lucas helped with the rest.

Then Melody came to the barn, carrying a large tray and blanket.

"Zara thought you might all like to have a picnic. It is
an unusually warm evening, and the stars are particularly
bright tonight."

As Melody led them outside, Lucas lagged behind.
After she spread out a blanket for them to sit on, Belle
brought her over to meet Lucas. He shook Melody's hand
awkwardly, standing as far away from her as possible.

"He's a little afraid of androids," Belle whispered
to Melody.

"Shall I tell him a few jokes?" Melody asked.

Melody stepped closer to Lucas, who froze in place.

"A duck walks into a chemist and says, 'Give me some
lip balm. Feel free to put it on my bill.'"

Belle held her breath. Would Lucas always be afraid
of Melody?

Lucas burst out laughing. "Ha! That's so bad."

Belle laughed too.

"Apparently, my work is done here," Melody said, as
she returned to putting out the picnic things.

The two families settled around the blanket as
Melody served everyone. Belle told the Walkers all about
what had happened the night before.

"Melody was the one who protected me from the
wolves," she said.

Lucas' eyes grew wide as he looked from Belle to Melody and back again. The purple rings around his brown eyes glowed in the starlight. Belle took a bite of turken leg, wiping the dripping juices from her chin. She had enjoyed entertaining everyone with her story.

As the night went on, laughter and light from the moon Phobos filled the air. Belle smiled as she watched her parents and the Walkers exchanging stories and having fun. This was the first moment that Belle had felt truly happy since moving to Mars. She was finally ready to call this strange red world her home.

Sol 112/Summer, Cycle 105

Tonight was pretty perfect. Lucas
and I fixed our project, and then we had
a fantastic picnic under the stars. Myra
talked about the constellations. Paddy told
us Martian fairy tales. Afterwards, Lucas
showed me how to make a catapult. Melody
and I taught him about Petripuffs. We might
just make him an android fan after all.

I think, even after everything that's
happened, I might just start to like it here on
Mars — maybe.

ABOUT THE AUTHOR

A.L. Collins learned a lot about writing from her teachers at Hamline University in Minnesota, USA. She has always loved reading science-fiction stories about other worlds and strange aliens. She enjoys creating and writing about new worlds, as well as envisioning what the future might look like. Since writing the Redworld series, she has collected a map of Mars that hangs in her living room and a rotating model of the red planet, which sits on her desk. When not writing, Collins enjoys spending her spare time reading and playing board games with her family. She lives near Seattle, Washington, USA, with her husband and five dogs.

• • • • • • • •

ABOUT THE ILLUSTRATOR

Tomislav Tikulin was born in Zagreb, Croatia. Tikulin has extensive experience creating digital artwork for book covers, posters, DVD jackets and production illustrations. Tomislav especially enjoys illustrating tales of science fiction, fantasy and scary stories. His work has also appeared in magazines such as *Fantasy & Science Fiction*, *Asimov's Science Fiction*, *Orson Scott Card's Intergalactic Medicine Show*, and *Analog Science Fiction & Fact*. Tomislav is also proud to say that his artwork has graced the covers of many books including Larry Niven's *The Ringworld Engineers*, Arthur C. Clarke's *Rendezvous With Rama* and Ray Bradbury's *Dandelion Wine* (50th anniversary edition).

:WHAT DO YOU THINK?:

1. Belle was often angry in this story. Why do you think she felt that way? What other ways could she have responded to her new life on Mars? How would you have felt if you were in Belle's place?

2. Mars is further from the Sun than Earth and has a much longer year. If you were born on Mars, how old would you be? What do you think the seasons would be like, and how would they be different from Earth's seasons?

3. Lucas wasn't very nice to Belle when they first met. Why do you think he behaved this way? If you were Lucas, how would you handle meeting new people?

4. If you could terraform a planet, write about what you would change so that humans could survive on it. Draw a map of your new planet and include everything needed for people to live there.

5. Lucas and the other children at Belle's new school make fun of Ta'al and don't play with her. Why do you think they treat her this way? Write about how you might react if you met an odd-looking alien.

:GLOSSARY:

binary something made of or having two parts

catamaran boat with two side-by-side hulls

claustrophobic feeling of being confined in a small or tight space

corrugated having parallel rows of folds, which look like waves when seen from the edge

desalination process of removing salt from seawater

hybrid plant or animal that has been bred from two different species

introvert shy person who keeps his or her thoughts and feelings to himself or herself

methane colourless, flammable gas produced by the decay of plant and animal matter

redundant dismissed from a job because the job is no longer needed

torso part of the body between the neck and waist, not including the arms